PENGUIN M

Fool

Jayanath Pati (1890–1939) was born in Sadipur village of Nawada subdivision of Gaya district, Bihar. After completing his intermediate (10+2), he cleared the exam to become a *mukhtar* (a lawyer knowledgeable in British laws during the colonial Raj in India) and set up a successful practice in Nawada. He was well versed in Urdu and Persian and knew Sanskrit, English, Bangla and Latin. His first novel, *Sunita* (1927), was about a woman who is married to an elderly man, the manuscript of which seems to be lost. His second novel, *Fool Bahadur*, was published on April Fool's Day in 1928 followed by his third novel, *Gadahnit*, in the same year.

Abhay K. from Nalanda, Bihar, is a poet, editor, translator, and the author of several poetry collections. His poems have appeared in over 100 literary magazines including *Poetry Salzburg Review* and *Asia Literary Review*, among others. His 'Earth Anthem' has been translated into over 150 languages and his translations of Kalidasa's *Meghaduta* and *Ritusamhara* from the Sanskrit won him the KLF Poetry Book of the Year Award (2020–21).

He received the SAARC Literary Award 2013 and was invited to record his poems at the Library of Congress, Washington, D.C., in 2018. His forthcoming poetry collection is titled In *Light of Africa*.

ALSO BY ABHAY K.

Poetry Collections
Enigmatic Love (2009)
Fallen Leaves of Autumn (2010)
Candling the Light (2011)
Remains (2012)
The Seduction of Delhi (2014)
The Eight-Eyed Lord of Kathmandu (2018)
The Prophecy of Brasilia (2018)
The Alphabets of Latin America (2020)
The Magic of Madagascar (2021)
Monsoon (2022)
Stray Poems (2022)
Celestial (2023)

Edited Books
CAPITALS (2017)
100 Great Indian Poems (2018)
100 More Great Indian Poems (2019)
New Brazilian Poems (2019)
100 Grandes Poemas da Índia (2019)
Cien Grandes Poemas de la India (2019)
100 Grandi Poesie Indiane (2019)
The Bloomsbury Anthology of Great Indian Poems (2020)
Tononkalo Indianina 100 Tsara Indrindra (2020)
100 Grands Poèmes Indiens (2022)
The Book of Bihari Literature (2022)

Translated Books
Meghaduta (2021)
Ritusamhara (2021)

Memoirs
River Valley to Silicon Valley (2007)

ADVANCE PRAISE FOR THE BOOK

'*Fool Bahadur* is a delightful sketch of a *mofussil* in late colonial times, warts and all. Set in Bihar Sharif, the novella takes us to the underbelly of the locale—a place rife with endless intrigues and dark, foolish ambitions. Dressed immaculately as a critical insider, Jayanath Pati puts a fictional spin on his own experiences as a law officer, decrying the heartless bearings of patriarchy, laying bare the illusions of feudalism and satirizing the corruption bred at large by colonial paraphernalia. In that sense, *Fool Bahadur* sits easily in the tradition of Balmukund Gupta, Fakir Mohan Senapati, and later, of Shrilal Shukla. Abhay K.'s apt translation, richly complemented by an exhaustive introduction, makes our first major foray into Magahi literature thoroughly wondrous and stimulating'—Gautam Choubey

'Sharp and satirical, the English translation of *Fool Bahadur* by Abhay K. is a compulsive read that remains contemporary even after the passage of almost a century. The caustic portrayal of mofussil life remains as relevant now as it was then'—Namita Gokhale

JAYANATH PATI

Fool Bahadur

Translated by Abhay K.

PENGUIN BOOKS

An imprint of Penguin Random House

PENGUIN BOOKS

USA | Canada | UK | Ireland | Australia
New Zealand | India | South Africa | China | Singapore

Penguin Books is part of the Penguin Random House group of companies
whose addresses can be found at global.penguinrandomhouse.com

Published by Penguin Random House India Pvt. Ltd
4th Floor, Capital Tower 1, MG Road,
Gurugram 122 002, Haryana, India

First published in the Magahi as फूल बहादुर 1928
Published in Penguin Books by Penguin Random House India 2024

Copyright © Jayanath Pati 2024
English translation and introduction copyright © Abhay K. 2024

ISBN 9780143463719

Typeset in Adobe Garamond Pro by Manipal Technologies Limited, Manipal
Printed at

www.penguin.co.in

To my mother, Dayawanti Devi, who taught me Magahi

TRANSLATOR'S NOTE

Surprised to learn that there is no written poem in Magahi
I run here and there, then sit down to write a poem in Magahi

I listen to the people in the street talking in Magahi
paying attention to their sounds and tones in Magahi

They twitter like birds day and night in Magahi
even their abuses sound sweet in Magahi

thik hai is thik hako, accha aa gaya is accha aa gelhu in
*   Magahi*
khana khaye is khana khailhu, chai piye is chaiya pilhu
*   in Magahi*

I go around the town looking for books in Magahi
I return home without finding a written word in Magahi

At home, I hear my mother say her prayers in Magahi
Hamar betake buddhi dehu bhagwan, he wants to write a
poem in Magahi.[*]

'Poetry,' wrote William Wordsworth, 'is the spontaneous overflow of powerful feelings: it takes its origin from emotion recollected in tranquillity.' When I wrote this poem in June 2020, it was, perhaps, in a whirlwind of emotions, or in a quest to reconnect with my roots through my mother tongue, Magahi. You will ask, 'What is this language that is Magahi?' It is believed that Buddha and Mahavira delivered their sermons in Magadhi Prakrit, which later gave birth to Magahi. Magadhi Prakrit was the official language of the Mauryan empire, and some of the edicts of Ashoka were composed in it. Written in the Brahmi script, it was the sacred language of Buddhism. Yet, Magahi officially ceased to be an independent language in India a long time ago. It was listed as a language in Bihar but has since then been grouped generically, under Hindi.

Magahi is spoken in the area south of the Ganges and east of the Son River across nine districts of Bihar, eight districts of Jharkhand and West Bengal's Malda district. There are around 20 million speakers of Magahi around the world.

---

[*] Thik hai: All well; Accha aa gaya: Well, you have arrived; Khana khaye: Did you eat?; Chai piye: Did you drink tea?; Hamar beta ke buddhi dehu bhagwan: God, give my son some sense

On a more personal note, I was born in the Nalanda district of Bihar and my mother speaks to me in Magahi, while my father used to speak in Hindi. When I came to study at Delhi University, people asked me if I spoke Bihari. I found this rather strange because I had no idea what they meant by 'Bihari'. All I knew were Magahi and Hindi. In fact, in the school syllabus, we had several Hindi stories and poems. Even English was a compulsory subject in high school and I had to learn poems such as Shakespeare's 'All the World's a Stage' and Wordsworth's 'Daffodils' by heart. Sadly, there was no mention of Magahi stories or poems. I studied Sanskrit in high school and learnt about the literature of ancient India, but I was not aware of the literary treasures in my mother tongue.

In fact, my ignorance was so profound that I thought that there was no written literature in Magahi, as I had never come across a single literary work in the language. But my ignorance was dispelled soon after I wrote this poem. People came up to me and made me aware of Magahi's rich literary heritage.

It took me almost a year to explore and locate Magahi folk tales, short stories and novels, and the treasures I found left me spellbound. Talking to various Magahi writers and poets, I was surprised to learn that the major works of Magahi literature had not been translated into English yet. I started collecting and translating poems and short stories from Magahi into English. I began by translating the very first Magahi short story, 'The Corner Mango Tree', by

Rabindra Kumar. It was during this time that I first came across Jayanath Pati's *Fool Bahadur*, which can be treated as the first Magahi novel, as not a single copy of *Sunita*, his first novel, is traceable. There were many attractions to the novel. Being a civil servant and from Nalanda myself, I was fascinated by it during my very first reading and immediately felt the need to take this classic piece to non-Magahi speakers around the world.

Before I talk more about the plot of the novel, let me take you back to ancient Magadha, its history, its language, Magadhi Prakrit, which later evolved into many languages including Magahi. Here, I am presenting a brief history of Magadha and the Magahi language, which is mainly based on my translation of parts of Sampati Aryani's valuable book, *Magahi-Bhasha aur Sahitya.**

Magadha: A Brief History

Bihar has a long history that dates back to the foundation of the *Mahajanapada* (great kingdom) of Magadha in southern Bihar, with its capital at Rajgriha (modern Rajgir) and later, at Pataliputra (modern Patna). Over the centuries, several dynasties ruled Magadha and gave rise to two of India's greatest empires—the Maurya and the Gupta empires that bore witness to great advancements in mathematics, astronomy, literature, philosophy, science,

---

* Sampati Aryani, *Magahi-Bhasha aur Sahitya*, Patna: Bihar Rashtrabhasha Parishad (1976).

statecraft, and the emergence of new religions such as Buddhism and Jainism.

Ancient Magadha and Its People

The vast expanse of ancient Magadha was to the south of the Ganges and north of the Vindhya mountains. It extended up to Mudgagiri (modern Munger) in the east and Charanadri (modern Chunar) in the west. Magadha does not find a mention in the Rigveda; however, there is a mention of the word 'Kikata', the dwelling place of non-Aryans, and their king, 'Pramagand'.

Kikata means those who do nothing. These people lent money to others and were famous as the rich moneylenders, and because of their wealth, they came to be known as 'mag' (one who lends money to earn interest) and the country, Magadha.

It becomes clear from later literary sources that Kikata makes reference to south Bihar or Magadha. The word 'Magadha' is mentioned in the Atharvaveda as a place where malaria was prevalent, and its people were referred to as 'Magadhi'. The kingdom of Magadha also finds a mention in the Yajurveda.

As the Aryans gradually moved across the country towards the east, they came into close contact with non-Aryans, who were defeated and forced to move southwards. Magadha was a forested land, where they took shelter. It became an eyesore for the Aryans, who had already settled in north Bihar and became the centre of their hatred, which continued for centuries, traces of which are still found today. To date, the south bank of the Ganges, where Magadha starts, is not considered sacred by the people of Mithila. Thus, historically, Magadha was considered a place where all kinds of libertine acts were permitted. Even the Aryans who settled and intermingled with the non-Aryans had a liberal, forward-looking and progressive outlook. The Aryans could never dominate Magadha, and its people never embraced the Aryan culture completely. Perhaps, that is why Magadha is portrayed in a bad light throughout Vedic literature, and perhaps, that's the reason why non-Brahmanical religions such as Buddhism and Jainism took root here and spread widely.

King Brihadratha is mentioned among the sixteen powerful kings in the Mahabharata. In *Rajgriha Mahatamya* of Vayu Purana, he is addressed as the King of Magadha and the father of Jarasandha. Magadha as a well-ordered state finds mention in the Valmiki Ramayana as well. Aryans could not keep their blood pure in eastern India, and the later kings of Magadha such as Jarasandha and Mahapadma Nanda were called Asur or Shudra.

The historical period of Magadha is divided into the Buddha Era, followed by Jaina, Maurya, Shunga, Gupta, Middle Ages, Moslem and English eras.

The history of Magadha begins with the ascent of King Bimbisara to the throne, followed by his son, Ajatshatru, who built a small fort (Pataligrama) near the Ganges River, and grandson, Udayin, who founded the city of Patliputra. Bimbisara belonged to the Shishunaga dynasty. The last king of this dynasty, Mahapadmananda, founded the Nanda dynasty, while Chandragupta Maurya killed the last Nanda king and established the Maurya dynasty.

Buddhism is Magadha's gift to India and the world. The two luminous disciples of Buddha, Maudgalyayana and Sariputra, who took Buddhism to new heights, hailed from Magadha. Jainism also flourished here and gave India a fresh line of thinking, free from Vedic rituals, religious dogma and a tendency for violence.

Magadha became a major power centre in the Indian subcontinent during the reign of the Maurya dynasty because of the intellect, wisdom and strategic thinking of its successive kings. The duo of Emperor Chandragupta Maurya and Chanakya posed a formidable pair of power and intellect that is rare in world history. Magadha remained a source of inspiration for a thousand years after the end of the Maurya dynasty.

Emperor Ashoka, who is hailed as one of the greatest emperors in the history of mankind, contributed a great deal to shaping world culture.

The Gupta period (4–6 CE) is known as the golden period in Indian history, which reached its zenith during the reign of Samudragupta, son of Chandragupta I, the founder of the Gupta dynasty. During the reign of his son, Chandragupta II (Vikramaditya), the empire witnessed the expansion and development of science, art and trade, and contact with foreign powers. The Chinese traveller, Faxian, visited Pataliputra in the early 5 CE and stayed for two years learning Sanskrit. Kumaragupta I, son of Chandragupta II, founded the great monastery of Nalanda between Pataliputra and Rajgriha, which became a famous centre of knowledge and learning for centuries until it started declining in the twelfth century. It greatly contributed to elevating India's historical, cultural and spiritual significance.

The Huns began to invade India (5–6 CE) during the reign of successive weak kings after Skandgupta of the Gupta dynasty, and thus, after a thousand years of being the capital of the Magadha empire, Pataliputra started witnessing a slow and gradual decline.

Gopala established a powerful kingdom uniting Bihar and Bengal in 743 CE, laying the foundation of the Pala dynasty, which reigned until 1023 CE. He and his son, Dharmapala, contributed greatly to the glory of Magadha. Palas built grand Buddhist temples and monasteries (Viharas)including the Somapura Mahavihara and Odantapuri, and patronized the great universities of Nalanda and Vikramashila. They also exerted a strong cultural influence in Tibet, as well as in Southeast Asia. Palas gradually lost control of north India as they were defeated by the Gurjara-Pratiharas, the Rashtrakutas and the Cholas. They were finally expelled in the twelfth century by the Senas, who were Hindus, ending the last Buddhist imperial power in the Indian subcontinent. This period also witnessed the end of patronage to the Buddhist monasteries such as Nalanda and frequent raids by Turks including one by Bakhtiyar Khalji which hastened the decline of Magadha. During 1200–1700, many rulers came and went, leaving Magadha in a state of flux. The

East India Company took over the reins of Bihar and Bengal in 1765. Bihar was separated from Bengal in 1912, and with the return of the capital of Bihar to Patna and the founding of Patna University, the Magadha and Magahi languages started witnessing a renaissance.

Magahi Language

Magahi belongs to the Indo-European group of languages. It has gradually developed from Sanskrit and Prakrit. Modern Indo-European languages are divided into external, middle and internal parts.* Magahi belongs to the eastern group of the external part of Indo-European languages along with Maithili, Bhojpuri (Magahi, Maithili and Bhojpuri are known as Bihari), Bangla, Odia and Assamese.

Buddha and his teachings played a key role in the development of Pali and Magadhi Prakrit as he refused to get his teachings translated into Sanskrit. Among the Prakrits, Magadhi Prakrit has a special place as the mother of many Eastern languages. Magadhi was the language of Magadha as well as Kashi, Koshal and Videh (north Bihar).

According to the linguist Suniti Kumar Chatterji, Buddha gave his sermons in Magadhi, which was later translated into Pali, a literary language based on an ancient Shauraseni Prakrit of the Madhyadesha (Ujjain to Mathura). Pali is incorrectly considered the language of Magadha or south Bihar; in fact, it would be more appropriate to call

---

* As per Sir George Abraham Grierson, who conducted the linguistic survey of India in 1898.

it an ancient form of western Hindi. It is because it has the predominance of *sa* in place of *sha* and *ra* in place of *la*. Magadhi, on the other hand, does not have either of these two attributes. Pali–Tripitaka has many Magadhi words, and that is why it is accepted that the original Tripitaka must have been in Magadhi. Magadhi was commonly used for the sermons in Buddhism and Jainism.

Magadhi was also the official language in the court of Ashoka. Dramatists began to write the dialogues of the princes and other important characters in Magadhi in their plays. The best example of Magadhi is the stone edicts of Ashoka found in Odisha, Uttar Pradesh and Bihar. According to the Chinese scholar Xuanzang, the same language was spoken in Bihar, Bengal and western Assam in the seventh century, and it was Magadhi Prakrit Apabhraṃśa. Magadhi Prakrit is therefore the mother of Magahi, Bhojpuri, Maithili, Odia, Bangla, Assamese and Halbic (Halbi, Kamar, Bhunjia and Nahari) languages spoken in southern Chhattisgarh. In due course of time, *dha* turned into *ha* and Magadhi turned into Magahi, which has a rich tradition of oral folk songs and folklore.

Magahi Literature

The written Maithili literature dates back to the fourteenth century, while in Bhojpuri, it's available from the fifteenth century onwards. However, no written literature is found from this period in Magahi. One of the reasons for this could be that the written Magahi literature was lost when the libraries of Odantapuri and Nalanda were burned towards the end of the twelfth century. Afterwards, the whole Magadha region came under the heavy influence of Moslem rule*, resulting in the renaming of Anga to Bihar, Patliputra to Patna and Odantapuri to Bihar Sharif. Persian became the court language—replacing the local languages and leaving very little room for the development of written Magahi literature. Conversely, a rich tradition of Magahi *lok sahitya* (folk literature) developed during this period marked by notable literary works such as the 'Song of Gopinath' and the 'Song of Lorik'. Thereafter, during the British period, English became the dominant language and the development of written Magahi literature found no patronage.

Written Magahi literature is divided into two periods:

1. Ancient literature, which includes the Siddha, Natha and Sant literature.
2. New literature, which includes contemporary literature published in the form of books, magazines, journals and other printed publications.

Ancient Magahi Literature

Siddha Literature

Let us delve into the earliest form of Magahi as it existed in Siddha literature (8–12 CE). The early Siddha, Sarahpada,

---

* Moslem rule in Bihar began with the invasion and ransacking of Odantapuri by Bakhtiyar Khalji in the twelfth century.

lived in Nalanda, while the other major eighty-four Siddhas lived in Magadha and wrote poetry in early Magahi. Major poets like Sarahpada and Bhusukupa wrote in Magahi.

The speakers of Assamese, Odia, Bangla, Bhojpuri, Maithili and even Hindi consider Siddha literature to be their early literature.

Natha Pantha Literature

After the Siddhas, the works of poets of the Natha sect, such as Gorakhnath, Bharthari or Bhratrihari, among others, gained prominence. The Nathas were mainly wandering bards. In many of Gorakhnath's popular books, the language used is not pure Magahi but contains many Magahi words.

Bharthari wrote books such as *Vairagya Shatakam, Shringar Shatakam* and *Niti Shatakam.* One of his *Barahmasas** has an almost modern form of Magahi.

Poet Jagnik wrote the epic poem 'Alha', which is still popular in different parts of north India.

Sant Sahitya

In the tradition of saint-poets, there are several who have composed in Magahi:

---

* Barahmasa, literally meaning the twelve months in a year, is a poetry genre themed around a woman longing for her absent lover and describing her feelings against the backdrop of the passage of months.

Dhani Dharamdas mainly composed poems in Awadhi, Braj Bhasha and Bhojpuri. However, there are many popular poems in Magahi attributed to him. Belvedere Printing Works, Prayag, published a dictionary of Dhani Dharamdas in 1923, which has his poems in Bhojpuri and Magahi. Dharamdas was not a resident of Magadha but had visited in the past along with his guru, Kabir.

Badridas used to live in Salimpur, near Patna. Many of his Magahi songs are popular and have been published as an anthology titled *Jhoomar Dildar* by Satyasudhakar Press, Patna City (1952).

Chandandas was a poet based in Jehanabad and was a friend of Badridas.

Amritdas's songs are included in the anthology *Jhoomar Dildar*.

Janharinath was born in Gaya and wrote *Lalit Ramayana* in Awadhi (1893). However, some of his songs are available in Magahi as well.

Apart from these, there are other saint-poets who wrote verses in Magahi. Baba Kadamdas, Baba Sohangdas, Baba Hemnath Das and Khangbahadur are some of the noted ones.

A Ramayana written by a washerman is popular in Nawada, and another handwritten by a potter has also been presented to the Bihar Rashtrabhasha Parishad, Patna.

According to Bharat Singh, the former head of the department of Magahi at Magadh University, a poet named Surajdas wrote the *Ramayana* in Magahi in 1480, much before Tulsidas wrote his *Ramcharitmanas* in

Awadhi. There were eighteen Ramayanas, two Qurans and three Bibles written in Magahi. Magahi words are found in Bharat Muni's *Natya Shastra*, Tulsidas's *Ramcharitmanas*, Jayasi's *Padmavat* and Kabir's works.

As per R.B. Pandey (1980), Magahi literature after the Siddhas can be divided into four periods:[*]

Charan period (1200–1500 CE)

The Charan period began with the conquest of north India by the Turkish invaders. During this period, the Charans or Bhatts propagated the idea of folklore, which started taking root in many locally spoken languages all over north India, including Magahi. There was no written tradition of folklore and they were transmitted orally. 'Aalha-Udal', 'Lorikayan', 'Sorthi-Brijbhar', 'Naykva', 'Kunwar Vijayi', 'Gopichand', 'Bharthari-Charitra', 'Chatri Chauhan' and 'Nunchar', to name a few, are some of the popular Magahi folklores.

Devotional period (1500–1800 CE)

After the Mughals replaced the Turks as the rulers of India, a new stream of devotional songs and stories gradually rose to prominence. During this period, folk songs of Sati Bihula, Nag Panchami, and songs related to Chhath, Shitla Devi, Satnarayan Baba, Tij, Anant-

[*] Lata Atreya, Smriti Singh and Rajesh Kumar, 'Magahi and Magadha: Language and People', G.J.I.S.S., Vol.3(2): 52–59 (March–April 2014).

Chaudas, Jitia and Godhan were developed. Folk songs such as 'Reshma', 'Raja Dholan' and 'Netua Dayal Singh', and the famous proverbs of Ghagh, Bhaddari and Dak became popular in Magahi.

Development period (1800–1900 CE)

The development period comprises the work done by English historians, linguists and archaeologists to create a genealogical history of Bihari languages (Magahi, Maithili and Bhojpuri) and their interrelations. Magahi grammar was written for the first time, including books such as (i) *Seven Grammars of the Dialects and Subdialects of the Bihari Language* by G.A. Grierson (1883–86) (ii) *A Comparative Dictionary of Bihari Language* by Rudolf Hoernle and Grierson (1889). In this period, for the first time, Magahi folklore and folk songs were also published, which had survived only in spoken form until then. The contribution of the Christian missionaries is admirable in this regard. They translated the Bible into Magahi which was kept at the Shrirampur Mission. A document written in Magahi by a Chero King in 1784 is safely preserved in a district court in Daltongunj as well.

Modern period (1900 CE–present day)

The modern period (1900 CE onwards) saw the consolidation of the importance of the Magahi language and literature with the publication of folklore, songs and other forms of vernacular literature. Magahi grammar books were written and published, including (i) *Magahi Vyakaran*, ed. by Christian Missionary Press, Calcutta, around 1943, in Kaithi script (ii) *Magahi Vyakaran*, authored by Rajendra Prasad Yodheya (1957) (iii) *Magahi Vyakaran-Kosh*, authored by Sampatti Aryani (1965) (iv) *Magahi Vyakaran*, authored by Rajeshwar Prasad Sinha 'Anshul' (1970) and (v) *Hindi aur Magahi ki Vyakaranik Sanrachna*, authored by Saroj Kumar Tripathi (1993).

Sheela Verma (1985) studied the structure of the Magahi verb and worked on the *Phonetics of Magahi* (2007). The linguistic study of Magahi also includes the following: (i) *Phonology and Morphology of Magahi Dialect*, authored by A.C. Sinha (1966) (ii) *Magahi Phonology: A Descriptive Study*, authored by Saryoo Prasad (2008) (iii) *Magahi kaa Bhasha Vaigyanik Mimansa*, authored by Kumar Rajiv Ranjan (2010) and (iv) *Magahi ki Sanyukt Kriyaaon kaa Bhasha Vaigyanik Adhyan*, authored by Kumar Indradev (2007).

In 1943, Magahi literature was officially recognized when two poems, 'Jagauni' and 'Chand', by Krishnadev Prasad were included in the poetry collection published by Patna University. Prasad was an advocate in the Patna High Court. He composed his poems in Magahi, which inspired others to create Magahi literature. His essay 'Magahi Language and Literature' is included in the *Collection of Fifteen Essays on Folk Language* by Rahul Sankrityayan. On the occasion of Magahi Sahitya Sammelan (Ekangarsarai, Patna) in 1957, Ramashankar Shastri published a booklet titled *Magahi*, which includes his thoughts on the Magahi language. In the same year, Rahul Sanskritayan edited and translated Sarhapada's *Dohakosha*, which was published by Bihar Rashtrabhasha Parishad, Patna.

There have been many publications in Magahi since then which can be divided into folk literature and high literature.

A. Folk literature

In folk literature, there are several booklets published that have folkloric and devotional songs and are popular among the Magahi-speaking people. Some notable works are:

1. *Girija-Girish-Charit* and *Umashankar-Vivah-Kirtan* by Sridhar Prasad Mishra. He has twenty-one more published books to his name.
2. Magahi proverbs, idioms, songs, dictionaries, etc.
3. A special issue of the Magahi journal *Bihan* containing popular Magahi folk songs.
4. *Magahi Sanskar Geet* or *Magahi Ritual Songs* (1962) by Bihar Rashtrabhasha Parishad.
5. *Jhanjh ki Jhanak*, a collection of Magahi folk songs edited by Munishwar Rai Munish. It has some very interesting songs.
6. *Magahi Idioms and Riddles* (1928) by Jayanath Pati and Mahavir Singh.
7. *Magahi Proverbs* by Umashankar Bhattacharya.
8. *Magahi Folklore and Folktales* (2008) by Sheela Verma.

B. High literature

Poetry

In the field of poetry, Ramprasad Pundarik's Magahi poems have special importance. They act as a bridge between folk literature and high literature. In 1952, his poems were published as an anthology titled *Pundarika-Ratnamalika*, which had his Hindi as well as Magahi poems. This anthology includes 'Sohar', 'Jantsari', 'Jhoomar', 'Barahmasa', 'Holi', 'Birha', 'Chaiti' and 'Kajra', to name a few. He has also translated the Srimad Bhagavad Gita into Magahi in tune with 'Biraha', 'Aalha', 'Kunwar Vijayi', 'Sohar' and the like. He is also credited with translating *Meghaduta* into Magahi.

Suresh Dube Saras's collection *Nihora* (1958), Ramsihasan Vidyarthi's poetry collection *Jagarna* (1967), Ram Prasad Singh's *Sarahpad* (1982), Shivprasad Lohani's *Lohani Satsai* (2003), Krishna Mohan Pyare's *Sabasin* (2005), Mathura Prasad Navin's *Akhir Kahiya Tak* (2011) and Manoj Kumar Kamal's *Magahi Guldasta* (2016) have also been published.

Drama

In 1960, Ramnandan's first historical drama *Kaumudi Mahotsav*, a play with three acts, was published. Later, *Nayagaon* by Shrikant Shastri, *Lafandar Bhagat* by Ramnandan, *Khaini* by Virendra Prasad, *Kanahiya ke Darad* (1985) and *Niranajana Ke Sant* (1999) by Keshav

Prasad Verma, *Fulwa* (1999) and *Narak Jinagi* (2002) by Sumant, *Bhauji* (2002) and *Kaput* (2010) by Siddhanath Sharma, and *Aankh ke Patti Khul Gel* (2005), a collection of Magahi street plays by Vasudev Prasad, among others were published.

Essays

'Manjar' and 'Murga aur Bihan' by Shivanandan Prasad, 'Parikarma' by Prof. Ramnandan, 'Aher' by Vishwanath Singh, 'Ghummakad ki Dayari' by Lakshman Prasad and 'Magahi Vyakaran' by Sampati Aryani, 'Magahi Bhasa Nibandhawali' (1984) by Ras Bihari Pandey and 'Galbat' (1997) by Shiv Prasad Lohani, among others, are some of the important essays published in Magahi.

Poetry

Among the Magahi poets, the first name that comes to mind is Krishnadev Prasad, who was not only the pioneer of Magahi poetry but also of Magahi literature. He first started translating poetry from English and Bangla into Magahi, including the poetry of Rabindranath Tagore, and later started writing his own poetry in Magahi. His poetry celebrates the beauty of nature and social life. Other prominent Magahi poets include Ramgopal Sharma Rudra, Govardhan Prasad 'Saday', Jagdish Narayan Chaube, Ramnandan, Ramnaresh Pathak, Ramchandra Sharma 'Kishore', Harishchandra Priyadarshi, Surendra

Prasad Tarun, Rajendra Yodheya, Ramsinhasan Vidyarthi and Mathura Prasad Naveen, to mention a few.

Here is a list of Magahi poetry collections published over the years:

1946 *Appan Gita* by Shrinandan Shali
1946 *Injor* by Yogeshwar Singh 'Yogesh'
1965 *Magahi Sanesh* by Kapildev Trivedi
1965 *Vasanti* by Ram Vilas Rajkan
1966 *Lohchutti* by Yogesh
      Jagarna by Ram Sinhasan Singh Vidyarthi
      Magahi Kundaliyan by Mahavir Dubey
      Magahi Tarang by Triveni Sharma Sudhakar
1968 *Rajanigandha* by Ramvilas Rajkan
1971 *Lahra* by Babulal Madhukar
1973 *Taras Uthal Jiyara* by Mahendra Prasad Shubhanshu
1974 *Anguri ke Daag* by Babulal Madhukar
1978 *Sanjhauti* by Govind Pyasa
1979 *Darkit Lor* by Ranjan Kumar Misra
1979 *Barahiya Golikand* by Mathura Prasad Navin
1979 *Dhibari* by Rajendra Pandey
1984 *Updesha Gatha* by Ramgopala 'Rudra'
1993 *Papihara* by Mahendra Prasad Dehati
1996 *Adhratiya ke Bansuri* by Kumari Radha
1998 *Dil ke Ghav* by Ghamandi Ram
2000 *Morhar ke Paar* by Harindra Vidyarthi
2003 *Lohani Satsai* by Shivprasad Lohani
2005 *Sabasin* by Krishna Mohan Pyare
2007 *Phalgu se Ganga* by Harindra Vidyarthi

2010 *Kavitayen* by Jayaram Singh

2011 *Akhir Kahiya Tak* by Mathura Prasad Navin

2016 *Magahi Guldasta* by Manoj Kumar Kamal

Magazines and Journals

The first among Magahi magazines and journals was *Tarun Tapasavi*, a magazine edited and published by Shrikant Shastri of Ekangarsarai, who started publishing Magahi prose for the first time. Later, it became a quarterly titled *Magadhi*, edited by Shrikant Shastri and Ramvriksha Singh 'Divya'. The same magazine was later published by the Magahi Parishad in Patna in 1952. In 1955, Shrikant Shastri and Thakur Rambalak Singh started the publication of another Magahi magazine. In 1955–56, *Mahan Magadha* was published by Srigopal Misra Kesari. However, the publication was discontinued after nine or ten issues. Afterwards, a new journal, *Bihan*, was started by Srikant Shastri and Ramnandan.

A number of Magahi writers have published their work in these magazines and journals, including Sarvashri Radhakrishna, Lakshmi Prasad Din, Maithilisaran Vidyarthi, Pushpa Aryani, Suresh Prasad Singh, Ramnanadan and Rabindra Kumar, among others. It is evident from these published stories in magazines and journals that the level of Magahi short-story writing has risen by leaps and bounds ever since.

The Magahi Akademi was established in 1981 and started publishing a journal titled *Niranjana*. Akashvani

Patna radio station offers one of the major platforms for the propagation and promotion of Magahi literature by organizing gatherings of Magahi poets and writers.

Novels

Jayanath Pati's two novels, *Sunita* and *Fool Bahadur,* are pioneering works in the field of Magahi novels.

His first novel, *Sunita*, was published in 1928 by Chitragupta Press in Gaya, Bihar. Very little remains of this book today, lost as it is, somewhere in the archives. After great effort, I was able to locate a review by S.K. Chatterji, which appeared in the *Modern Review* in April 1928, Calcutta.

Modern Review, April 1928,
Vol. 43, p. 430

MAGAHI (BIHARI)
SUNITA: By Babu Jayanath Pati, Mukhtear, Nawada, South Bihar: Printed at the Chitragupta Press.
Gaya: 1928, p. 18, Price Two Annas.

Babu Jayanath Pati is a well-known Mukhtear of South Bihar and an accomplished scholar and linguist who does not disdain his mother tongue. We welcome this little story from him as one of the first publications of its kind in the speech of South Bihar, which is current among a population of over six million who have already accepted Hindi as their literary language. The story is a slight one, showing the evils of marrying young girls to old husbands. The heroine runs away with a young man, her childhood friend, and a great social evil is, in this way, exposed. The picture of some aspects of society in the Magadha land painted here is no doubt faithful, but there is not much characterization.

The value of this little work is primarily linguistic, but we hope the author will give us longer, equally faithful, and preferably more pleasing pictures of life and society in South Bihar. An attempt like the present one is sure to be remembered among future students of the Indian language and of social ethnology for the linguistic and social material it preserves. Chapbooks and popular books of verse are sometimes printed in Magahi for the masses who do not feel at home in High Hindi or who love the accents of their mother tongue more than that of the speech of the law court and the school, but only through a conscious literary effort like the present one, can a neglected language take a stand against the danger of being swept away.

It is perhaps too late in the day to think of creating new literature in Magahi, especially when its speakers, both educated and uneducated, have no sense of pride in it and are seemingly a little ashamed of their 'little language' which they are making haste to substitute by an indifferent kind of Hindi, a mixture of High Hindi and Awadhi. But some Magahi writers can lay open for us the soul of the Magahi people through their works (poems, dramas, or novels) in their own language, which would certainly add a new world to the rich and varied domain of Indian literature. And Mr Jayanath Pati, scholar, man of affairs, and lover of his people and his language, can very well be that Magahi writer.

S. K. C

Coming back to *Fool Bahadur*, Jayanath Pati's second novel, was published in the same year. As I mentioned before, copies of *Sunita* are not available any more. Therefore, *Fool Bahadur* can be considered the first Magahi novel today. Many of his other works such as *Gadahnit* are also not available. *Fool Bahadur* is his only surviving work.

Originally published on 1 April 1928 (April Fool's Day), a day of practical jokes and hoaxes, *Fool Bahadur* is a satire. The protagonist of the novel, Samlal, is made a fool of on 1 April with the bestowal of the fake title of 'Rai Bahadur' by pranksters.

As per the biography provided in the book, Pati was born in Sadipur village of Nawada subdivision of Gaya district of Bihar in 1890, twenty-one years after the birth of Mahatma Gandhi, and a decade after the birth of Munshi Premchand, a pioneer of Hindi and Urdu social fiction, was born. His father's name was Devaki Lal. He was sincere in his studies, and after completing his intermediate (10+2), cleared the exam to become a mukhtar (a lawyer well versed in British laws during the colonial Raj in India).

His practice took off, and he turned out to be a successful mukhtar in Nawada. He was well versed in Urdu and Persian and knew Sanskrit, English, Bangla and Latin. He was deeply interested in religious discourse. He also took part in the Swaraj (self-rule) movement led by Gandhi. In 1931, he was imprisoned for breaking the salt law. Earlier, mukhtars were not allowed to take up cases pertaining to revenue matters, and it was because of his efforts that mukhtars were permitted to argue revenue cases later. He was highly regarded by the mukhtars across the whole of Bihar. He passed away on 21 September 1939 in Patna due to typhoid, and was survived by three daughters and a son.

Here is my translation of the excerpts from the book review written by Ram Nandan for the 1974 edition of *Fool Bahadur*, published in the literary magazine *Bihan* (Dawn) by Ghanshyam Press:

Jayanath Pati wanted to take Magahi to the same height as Hindi or Bangla. To achieve this, he wanted to write as many books as possible and get them published. It seems he could not do much, however, he was able to write four books, as per the available records. His first novel was titled *Sunita*. It was named after Suniti Kumar Chatterji, a well-known scholar of Bangla and a world-famous linguist, as it was his book, *The Origin and Development of Bengali Language*, that inspired Jayanath Pati to revive and nurture Magahi. His third book was titled *Gadahnit*, while his fourth book was titled *Swaraj*, in which the Law of the Government of India in 1936 was written in Magahi.

He further adds,

> The first edition of *Fool Bahadur* was published in a four-page crown size. There was an image of a joker on the front cover who is dressed in a western suit, is ringing a bell with his right hand, and is holding a life-size paper cut-out in his left hand in which 'Fool Bahadur' is inscribed in large font. On the image, it is written *not for women and children*, and below it, *the second Magahi novel*. Below the image is the writer's name, Jayanath Pati. Price–three anna. It is evident from the above line that in those days, women and children were not permitted to read novels, although there was nothing inappropriate or lurid written in them.

Chatterji has also referred to *Fool Bahadur* as a satire. A mukhtar of Bihar Sharif, Samlal, is a devious man, determined to become a Rai Bahadur by hook or by crook. This satirical plot criticizes the rampant corruption among the judiciary and bureaucracy during those times. Though the book is in Magahi, there is no *anchalik* (regional) imprint on it. This novel does not depict the rural society of Bihar Sharif and its surrounding areas; rather, it depicts its urban milieu, and specifically, the life revolving around the court and judiciary in British-occupied Bihar.

Pati, in his 'Foreword to the First Edition' of *Fool Bahadur*, writes:

The way the readers have welcomed *Sunita* with respect and the way Suniti Kumar Chatterji has reviewed the book with such love in a well-known monthly literary journal, my courage has certainly gone up manifold. I believe his kindness towards Magahi will not diminish, and here I am with a second book for him. Certainly, there are shortcomings in it, and all endeavours will be made to do away with them.

Some of my Bhumihar (landowning Brahmins) brothers have gotten angry with me thinking that their caste has been portrayed in a poor light in *Sunita*. I would like to plead with them that I never had such intentions. The social evil that has been portrayed in it is no doubt prevalent, and it should be condemned regardless. Someone or another has to bear the brunt. In *Fool Bahadur*, it is a Lala (*Kayastha*)* who has borne the brunt. And in *Gadahnit*, some other caste will bear the brunt.

I had expected more criticism in the book review, but perhaps due to the bond of love that had formed during the first meeting, he conveyed his criticism to me discreetly. I have been nurturing the thought of enriching my mother tongue for the last twenty years, but because of a paucity of funds, I could not do it. There are hundreds of books ready, and many are on

---

* Land registrar.

the verge of completion, but how does one get them published? Last year, after reading the criticism of my beloved in *The Origin and Development of the Bengali Language*, I decided that lying low and hiding would not work and life would soon end without achieving much if I remained tangled in mundane matters. As a result, *Sunita* was written within three to four days and sent to print, and it was published so hurriedly that it was not even proofread. But because of people's kindness, I have been spared the criticism. I have been told indirectly that I should have begun with some good topic; however, I just want to say that there is hardly any place for my mother tongue to even sit, but whenever I have stood with the thought of treating her as a sister, I feel it needs some cleaning up first. If in the process some dust particles fall from it, it requires that, as a fellow man and friend, one be tolerant, and I am glad that he has discharged his duties elegantly. For all those who are spurning me, I would like to assure them that the shortcomings were limited to only one book and I will be more diligent in my next novel, *Gadahnit*, and will not give a reason to complain, and to further enrich my mother tongue, I will try to get the following books published—

1. *Panch Hajar Varash Mein Phool Ke Sugandh*: It means the presentation of hymns from the Rigveda and key mantras into Magahi. Besides that, a comparison of commentaries on them was published in German, French, English and Sanskrit.

2. *Magahi Ramayana*: It is very popular in our area and I'm getting it written.

3. *Sadhe Tin Hajar Varash Ke Sugandhit Phool* (Magahi translation of *Parsi Gatha*): It is also being completed.

4. *Magahi Mahabharata*

5. *Magahi Bhagwata*: It's ready

6. *Magahi Ke Bhasha-Vaigyanik Tatva*

7. *Magahi Me Budhi-Mamma*: An anthology of popular Magahi tales

8. *Magahi Kahavat*: Has been collected by a Bengali gentleman

9. *Bharatvarsh Ke Purana Haal*: As per my research

10. *Magahi Quran*

11. *Mohhamed Saheb Ke Jivani,* etc.

Many of these will not be completed during my lifetime; for this, I have deposited some money in the bank, so that after some time a good sum gets collected from the interest and whoever is its trustee can further make efforts to enrich Magahi in the future. Bangla and Hindi have evolved in the past fifty to 100 years. It won't be too long for Magahi. I'm afraid of one thing—that Hindi (or mixed Hindustani) should not gobble up Magahi. However, as long as the British Raj is here, it is not possible to educate everyone, and I am hopeful that because of this, the Magahi speakers who are illiterate will not forget or abandon their language. It will not prevent us from achieving Swaraj, but at the

same time, we will keep making efforts to give Magahi
its due place before the unruly sun sets over the British
empire.

J.P.

Nawada

1 April 1928

Since the publication of *Fool Bahadur* in 1928, several
novels have been published in Magahi in the past 100 years:

1928 *Sunita* by Jayanath Pati
     Fool Bahadur by Jayanath Pati
     Gadahnit by Jayanath Pati
1958 *Samasya* by Ram Prasad Singh
     Barabar ke Tarhatti Mein by Ram Prasad Singh
     Sarad Rajkumar by Ram Prasad Singh
     Medha by Ram Prasad Singh
1962 *Visheshra* by Rajendra Kumar Yodheya
1965 *Aadmi ka Devta* by Ramnandan
1968 *Ramratiya* by Babulal Madhukar
1969 *Monamimma* by Dwarka Prasad
1977 *Sanwali* by Shashibhusan Upadhayay Madhukar
1978 *Godna* by Srikant Shastri
     Saklya by Chandrashekhar Sharma
     Siddhartha by Chandrashekhar Sharma
     Haya Re U Din by Chandrashekhar Sharma
     Chutaki Bhar Senur by Satendra Jamalpuri
1980 *Accharang* by Prof. Ramnaresh Prasad Verma

1988 *Bas Ekke Rah* by Kedar 'Ajey'
1992 *Narag Sarag Dharati* by Ram Prasad Singh
1995 *Dhumail Dhoti* by Ram Vilas Rajkan
       Prani Mahasangh by Munilal Sinha 'Sisam'
2001 *Alganthwa* by Babulal Madhukar
2004 *Babuani Ainthan Chhoda* by Acharya Sachidanand
2005 *Baba Matokhar Das* by Parmeshwari Singh 'Anpadh'
       Gochar ke Rang: Goru-Gorkhiyan ke Sang by Munilal
          Sinha 'Sisam'
       Untiswan Vyas by Rambabu Singh Lamgoda
       Tun-Tunmei-Tun by Rambabu Singh Lamgoda
2006 *Shalish* by Parmeshwari
2011 *Tara* by Ramnarayan Singh aka Pasar Babu
2018 *Khanti Kikatiya* by Ashwani Kumar Pankaj
2022 *Pension ke Batasha* by Omprakash Jamuar

It is evident that Magahi language and literature have been witnessing an upward spiral during the past century—a number of important literary works from other languages have also been translated into Magahi.

A collection of 100 Magahi short stories and 100 great Magahi poems published over the past 100 years is also being compiled.

I hope the publication of *Fool Bahadur* in an English translation will bring greater attention to the rich world of Magahi literature and inspire more translations of literary works in Magahi in the years to come.

Abhay K.

References

Aryani, Sampati. 1976. *Magahi Bhasha aur Sahitya*. Patna: Bihar Rashtrabhasha Parishad.

Pandey, R.B. 1980. *Magahi Bhasha ka Itihas*. Gaya: Lok Sahitya Sagar.

Shrotriya, Dhananjay, ed. 2012. *Magahi Bhasa ka Itihas evam Iski Disha aur Dasha*. Patna: Lalit Prakashan.

Sinha, Arun. 2022. Magahi, a Language That Refuses to Die despite Hindi Imperialism. Southfirst, 24 November.

CHAPTER 1

Babu Samlal was a mukhtar* of some repute in Bihar Sharif, but he had earned his fame and fortune by stooping rather low in his professional and personal conduct. His father was a driver and his *fufa*† was a schoolteacher, who persuaded him to study till middle school. After that, he worked as a cook at one of the mukhtars' households.

Eventually, he took the exam to become a mukhtar himself and managed to pass after three failed attempts. He was a clever man, and he was scandalous too. He somehow got by with his work as a mukhtar.

He lent some money to Suganlal, a Kayastha but when Suganlal failed to repay his debt, he mortgaged the man's home, got it registered in his name, built it up a few stories

---

* A legal practitioner in a lower court in India during the British Raj in the nineteenth and early twentieth century.
† Paternal aunt's husband.

and got Suganlal to work as his cook in the house! Such was his character.

Normally, all government servants demand attention and are susceptible to flattery. This tendency can be attributed to the foreign rule including the British in India. Samlal possessed a good deal of these qualities and kept his bosses happy, which made the rich and influential of the town envy him. In his profession, there was no growth without resorting to flattery and backbiting.

It so happened that in March 1911, Maulavi Mojjafer Nawab, Sub-Divisional Officer* (SDO) Manbhum, was transferred to Bihar Sharif.† Haldhar Singh, the circle officer,‡ had already been working there for about a year.

For quite some time, Samlal nurtured the ambition of becoming a Rai Bahadur.§ Although he was well aware that he did not merit the post, he had complete faith in his art of flattery.

A day before the expected time of the arrival of the new SDO, he reached Kiul Railway Station and busied himself with making arrangements to welcome the new SDO at

---

* A sub-divisional officer, also known as assistant collector, sub-collector, assistant commissioner, sub-divisional magistrate or revenue divisional officer, is an administrative officer of a sub-division within an Indian district, exercising executive, revenue, and magisterial duties.
† A town located 74 km south-east of Patna, the capital of the state of Bihar, which now serves as the headquarter of Nalanda district.
‡ A circle officer or SDPO is responsible for overseeing law and order, crime prevention, and investigation within a designated area known as a police subdivision.
§ A title of honour bestowed during British rule in India to individuals for outstanding service or acts of public welfare to the Empire.

a popular eating joint. The next day, when SDO Nawab Saheb alighted from the train at 7 p.m., Samlal introduced himself and offered his salutations to him. He then went on to inform him that the connecting train to Bihar Sharif was delayed and entreated him to have some snacks while he waited.

Nawab Saheb politely refused, adding that he did not feel like eating anything at the moment. Samlal made gentle protestations that he had specially come to welcome him from far away and had already made all the arrangements for the refreshments. This irked Nawab Saheb a little; however, being from a noble family, he refrained from saying anything rude to Samlal.

He spoke in Urdu:

'Please excuse me, at this moment. After a long train journey, I feel queasy. It seems that whatever I've eaten earlier has not been digested yet.'

Samlal looked around here and there, then touched the Nawab's feet swiftly. 'Sir, please have mercy on me.'

Nawab Saheb had met many supplicants before, but never such a rare one. Finally, he gave in to Samlal's entreaties. He thought to himself about how Samlal would not budge since he had come all the way from Bihar Sharif just to receive him, and it would be discourteous to turn him down. So he conceded his demand and decided to go with him.

At last, they went to a nearby eating joint after asking their assistants to look after the luggage. The waiter brought some biscuits, tea and eggs for Nawab Saheb.

As Mukhtar Samlal sat across the table, the Nawab requested some food to be brought for him too. Samlal protested, saying that he was a pure vegetarian. Despite the Nawab's appeals, Samlal declined to eat anything. Finally, the Nawab asked for some fruits to be brought. Samlal was grateful for the bananas and oranges that were placed before him along with hot cups of tea on a separate table next to where the Nawab was eating.

The Nawab chatted as they ate. 'Tell me about Bihar Sharif,' he said. 'What kind of a place is it? And how are the mukhtars there?'

'They are all gentlemen,' said Samlal.

Nawab Saheb: Are they all advocates?

He said, 'Yes, there are a few advocates too.'

Nawab Saheb: Is there cooperation and harmony among the mukhtars and the advocates?

Samlal: Oh, certainly there is! However, there is animosity and bad blood among the mukhtars themselves.

Nawab Saheb: Why?

Samlal: For no reason in particular.

Nawab Saheb: How is that possible?

Samlal: They all envy me. I live in a mansion. I always have five to ten thousand rupees as my bank balance. They all desire the same thing. Hakims like me more than others.

Nawab Saheb: What about the honorary magistrates?

Samlal: Yes, sir, there are a few honorary magistrates too.

Nawab Saheb: How are they in their conduct?

Samlal: Just the same as others. But they consider themselves a class apart.

Nawab Saheb: Why?

Samlal: They are all influential people; what can I say about them?

Nawab Saheb: Please rest assured. I will never land you in any trouble. You can tell me.

Samlal: Sir, if you insist, I must tell you. Except for a couple of them, the rest take bribes. They have made a lot of money.

Nawab Saheb: Tell me more about them. Are they responsible?

Samlal: Barring the graduates, these less educated honorary magistrates take ten rupees from one of the disputing parties and pronounce the verdict in their favour, but if the second party involved offers five rupees more than the first one, the verdict goes in the latter's favour. Magistrates with such a mindset pass judgment on cases that involve clients whose net worth is several thousand, so that they occasionally may earn Rs 100 or 50 in cash or kind.

Nawab Saheb: Do the SDO and others know about it?

Samlal: How would they not know?

Nawab Saheb: So why do they turn a blind eye and assign cases to them?

Samlal: During the previous SDO, Gudiyar Sahib's tenure, he stopped sending cases to them. They then pleaded with him a great deal, and eventually, some petty cases were assigned to them. But when he left, the status quo returned.

Nawab Saheb: The situation here is very bad. Bribery and cruelty are prevalent among the police and officialdom. Now even the higher officials engage in the same. The very foundation of the state has been infested with termites. They should be eradicated.

Samlal: No comments, sir!

Nawab Saheb: Alright!

After having tea, the Nawab wiped his mouth with a handkerchief, and while coming out of the eatery, handed over the bill to his servant, asking him to settle it.

Samlal said, 'It's not needed, sir. It has already been taken care of.'

Chatting, they walked towards the train platform.

Nawab Saheb (in Urdu): Listen, I feel very sorry to hear about the situation here.

Samlal: They are all my friends, sir. They should not be dealt with severely.

Nawab Saheb: No, I'm not bad-mouthing anyone. Rest assured, I'm from a noble family myself.

Samlal: Yes, sir, that's evident.

Nawab Saheb: The late Nawab Wajad Ali Shah was my ancestor.

Samlal: Certainly, sir, your mannerisms speak volumes about you.

Nawab Saheb: My great-great maternal grandpa was his grandson.

Much of what the Nawab said was inexplicable to Samlal, but he nodded his head seriously, smiling at all the right places. 'That's great, sir,' he said enthusiastically.

The Nawab said, 'Sometimes, my blood boils. With how the Sultanate has been annexed deceitfully by the British, the defeat of Turkey, and how we are being weakened by the Arab world, God will certainly dispense justice.'

Samlal: Yes, he certainly will.

It was time for the train to arrive. Passengers started walking towards the platform with their baggage. Nawab Saheb instructed his servants to take his baggage to the platform.

CHAPTER 2

The train arrived. All the passengers began to load their luggage and board the train. Nawab Saheb's assistants started to load his luggage too. Meanwhile, a woman greeted Samlal from the gangway of the train compartment. He greeted her back and gestured towards the SDO with his eyes, suggesting he was the one departing. The woman hid herself, but Nawab Saheb saw her. However, he pretended not to have seen her and boarded the train. Samlal also got into the same cabin as him.

As the train left the station, Nawab Saheb, reclining on the berth, spoke (in Urdu), 'Who was that woman who greeted you?'

Samlal: She is a courtesan from Bihar Sharif. Once, I had helped her in a case under Section 60.*

---

* As per Section 60 of the Indian Penal Code 1860 in every case in which an offender is punishable with imprisonment which may be of either description, it shall be competent to the Court which sentences such offender to direct in

The Nawab nodded knowledgeably. 'The police are excessive at times,' he said. 'At the slightest disagreement, they file cases against dissenters under Section 60.'

'That was not the case here,' said Samlal.

'Then what was the matter?'

'It was a matter of legal dispute, sir. I am unsure whether I should tell you about it,' hesitated Samlal. The Nawab assured him, 'You'll not get into any trouble because of me. You're an affable man and I like such people.'

Samlal smiled and said, 'My life is in your hands hereafter, sir.'

Nawab Saheb: Don't worry!

'Her name is Naseeban,' said Samlal. 'They say that she is still a virgin. Babu Haldhar Singh is a circle officer in Bihar Sharif. When he saw Naseeban, he tried several times to talk her into visiting him, but she did not agree. He got angry and sought help from his friend, Nitneshwar Babu, the police inspector, who got a case registered against her under Section 60. Babu Haldhar Singh did all he could to bring the case under his jurisdiction. She hired me as a mukhtar knowing that I was his friend. Somehow, I managed to get her released.'

Nawab Saheb appeared to be impressed. He straightened up from his reclining position and said, 'I see. You seem to be quite an interesting fellow. I had thought

---

the sentence that such imprisonment shall be wholly rigorous, or that such imprisonment shall be wholly simple, or that any part of such imprisonment shall be rigorous and the rest simple.

that such a long journey would be a dry affair. But you are a godsend for me.'

Samlal: Sir, I am humbled.

Nawab Saheb extended his hand and so did Samlal. Clasping his hand, Nawab Saheb said, 'Consider me as your friend.'

Samlal: As it pleases you, sir. I'm your humble servant.

Nawab Saheb: Just one thing, please forgive my impoliteness.

Samlal: Sir, you're embarrassing me.

Nawab Saheb: If possible, please call Naseeban here so we can chit-chat during the rest of the journey. However, please don't tell her that I'm the new SDO.

Samlal felt slightly uneasy at this order. But he agreed to do so when the train halted at the next station. He worried that the circle offices' men would be lurking around.

Nawab Saheb asked if she was the mistress of one of the officers.

'No, she is not a mistress,' said Samlal. 'She is, after all, a courtesan! Things are done discreetly here and she is still a novice.'

Nawab Saheb got restless and said, 'Please don't delay further, you must go at once.'

When the train stopped at Mokama, Samlal got off and went into Naseeban's wagon and asked her to follow him. But Naseeban refused to accompany him, pointing out that it would bring on Haldhar Singh's ire. Despite Samlal's many requests, she didn't go with him and he went back to the Nawab alone. Nawab Saheb was desperately strolling

back and forth in front of Naseeban's compartment. He
sought to bribe her with a ten rupee note via Samlal and
even suggested intimidation.

Somehow, Samlal managed to convince Naseeban and
brought her along with him to the first-class compartment.
Upon seeing Naseeban alight from her compartment and
walk towards the first class, Nawab Saheb quickly got
onto the train and pretended to read the newspaper while
reclining on his berth.

When Naseeban came, he put down the newspaper,
and bearing a solemn look on his face, said, 'Please have a
seat, *Bai-jaan*."

He switched on the fan and chatted with her the whole
journey. When the train was two or three stations from its
final destination, he sent Naseeban back to her carriage.

---

* A term of endearment to address courtesans.

CHAPTER 3

Within a few days of assuming charge as the new SDO, Nawab Saheb began to assign fewer cases to the honorary magistrates. Only those cases under Section 34* or 60 were occasionally assigned to them, and if not, he either tried to dispose of them himself or assigned them to his two deputies. Babu Haldhar Singh was sent on field duty and given other miscellaneous work. Killing two birds with one stone, Nawab Saheb curbed the power of honorary magistrates and got more time to spend with Naseeban.

For a couple of months, Babu Haldhar Singh somehow managed to carry out the fieldwork assigned to him, but with the onset of the monsoon, he felt that his nature of work could take a toll on his health and prove fatal for him.

---

* Section 34 of the Indian Penal Code 1860 deals with criminal acts done by several persons in furtherance of common intention.

So, one day, he came to Nawab Saheb's office to discuss this matter. After beating about the bush, he came to the point.

'Although the number of cases has come down of late due to good governance, we are still burdened with work,' he said. The Nawab responded, 'The workload of *khas mahal** has increased. But the investigation of matters pertaining to *sar jamin*† has considerably reduced.'

Singh Ji persisted. 'The work of khas mahal, delegated to me by Saheb himself, is not difficult at all, but to go about surveying every piece of disputed land is really tedious. Earlier, this work was done by the honorary magistrates.'

'I've decided that, as far as possible, I will not assign such important matters of dispute to anyone and everyone,' said the Nawab. 'It is the poor petitioners who suffer the most.'

'It's an open secret that among the existing lot, very few are honest,' said Singh. The Nawab agreed.

'Therein lies the problem,' he said. 'If the cases were to be assigned to them alone, the others would be dispirited and offended without any rhyme or reason.'

Singh was exasperated. 'To what extent can this be prevented? Everyone reeks of bribery. When some judges of the high court are being openly criticized, what can be expected of these poor souls?' he said.

---

* Private land.
† Public land.

The Nawab pointed out that it was a matter for the government to resolve. 'But,' he said, 'if the problem persists, people often find a remedy themselves. Whatever little powers we have within our jurisdiction, we must exercise them fairly.'

Singh Ji: What can we do? Police accepting bribes is very disgraceful, barring a handful of them who are honest, the rest suck the blood of the *ryots*[*] like leeches. The government—doesn't it know what's going on? How can they be restrained? I don't think we can do anything about it.

Nawab Saheb was angry now. 'This is all rubbish,' he said. 'Either the government does not know who is in control here, or if they do, they choose not to act or pay attention. Take, for instance, the post office personnel—they draw a meagre salary, yet accepting bribes is not rampant among them. What could be the reason? You would say that they don't have much power. That's absolutely not correct. They deal with transfers of money all the time, delivering and receiving letters; if they wish, they can take bribes while discharging their duties. However, in the postal department, officers have greater trust in the public. As soon as someone lodges even a minor complaint, an investigation is carried out without delay, and punishment is meted out. Considering that their complaint might lead to the loss of livelihood of the concerned official, people do not complain unless they find themselves helpless. If some

---

[*] An Indian peasant or tenant farmer.

ill-tempered person complains over trifles, his complaints are simply rubbished. Now let us take the instance of the government's right hand, the police! If someone lodges an anonymous complaint against the police, no action is taken; but if an influential person files a complaint, then the matter is investigated by a magistrate of the first order and a witness is sought to prove the complaint in its entirety. Out of fear, no one is easily convinced to be a witness. If someone from one's own kith or kin becomes the witness, then the said person's account is considered null and void, and if at all a stranger becomes the witness, it is mostly because they are intimidated into doing so. So, if we trust people like the post office does, I wonder if that would work. Moreover, the authority of the government will be at risk. If the elixir of love cannot keep the tree alive, how long can it be saved from the worm of dread and authority?'

Singh Ji: You did not ponder over the fact that the *daroga** is entrusted with so much power, which is not any less than the authority given to us, or perhaps, it is far more. In that case, some measures must be taken to stop their greed on humanitarian grounds. Besides, there is a prevalent notion that whoever joins the police force becomes corrupt.

Nawab Saheb: I don't think that's true. A daroga gets Rs 50 as remuneration in the beginning, though he expects Rs 100, and if he performs his duty well, he can get

---

* Police sub-inspector.

promoted to the rank of inspector, deputy superintendent of police, and so on. Also, there is a general misconception that, had the said person been working in another part of the country, he would draw a decent salary and be leading a better life. In that case, if the corrupt police are dealt with strictly and the complaints are addressed expeditiously, they can be resolved in a very short time. At least it can be observed in one or two districts how daroga and *jamadar** function and this may help change our perception of them. It will take a long time to bring about the change using some of the unrealistic methods you talk about; one may encounter more difficulties than can be imagined at this moment. I have been thinking for quite some time now that the best solution would be to appoint deputies[†] in place of darogas. Despite holding a degree and earning decent remuneration, many have started taking bribes by virtue of their position. That's why I think that deputies should be appointed to every police station and that their rank and salary should be uniform.

Singh Ji: Won't the expenditure grow manifold?

'Not more than the 60 crores we spend now,' said Nawab Saheb. 'That's the amount of money spent in purchasing weapons and fighting imaginary enemies. Is it just that while no one is allowed from outside the borders, intrusion is thwarted, cannons and fighter jets are maintained for this purpose, and within the country, a

---

[*] A junior police officer.
[†] Deputies here refers to SDOs.

pack of colonial dogs are let loose on peasants to tear their
bones and muscles? How wonderful it would be if guns
and cannons were removed from the border and all the
restrictions imposed upon Indians to possess weapons were
lifted. Once again, blood will begin to flow in the veins of
a dead Hindustan. Have you ever seen a plant sheltered in
a room from stormy winds and sunlight grow and flower?
Moreover, it is Britain that will benefit more from this
than anyone else. If we don't fight, where will they find
people like Mir Jafar and Mir Qasim?'

'This is not feasible,' said Singh. 'The government,
whether from its own volition or because of its misplaced
thinking, will not spend such a huge sum, and will not
withdraw cannons and cannonballs from the border areas.'

'Taxes should be increased,' argued the Nawab. 'I
understand that on average one has to pay Rs 200 for each
case. If an additional Rs 10 is charged for filing an FIR
or Rs 15 as the court fee, then the monthly salary of the
deputies can automatically be paid out of it. The poor can
be spared the fee. There would be a few who would readily
pay, given the fact that it would help stop the practice of
bribery. By raising the court fees, the salary can be further
increased. For cases pertaining to land disputes, the court
can pass a law whereby, upon receiving the application,
a copy of the same should be sent to the other party in
dispute.'

Singh Ji: For making copies of documents of land titles
at the court, accepting bribes is already existent. In Bokaro,
all kinds of forged documents are prepared. If three carbon

copies could be obtained, where one copy each is given to the two parties in dispute and one is kept for the court's record, then all the problems could be solved.

Nawab Saheb: I am writing a book highlighting these matters, and I wish to present it before the government. But I wonder, who would listen to me?

Singh Ji: If they don't listen, they will suffer themselves.

Nawab Saheb: They are already suffering.

Singh Ji: I should at least be spared the trouble during the rainy season. In fact, honorary magistrates should be allotted work in areas under their jurisdiction.

Nawab Saheb: What can I do, my conscience is shaken . . .

Singh Ji: Why should they be kept in service at all then?

Nawab Saheb: As a matter of fact, those who are honest do not go around sweet-talking, and the ones who have earned the titles have done so by resorting to the art of flattery before their senior officers.

Singh Ji: It all appears inscrutable to me.

'Let it continue for a while,' said the Nawab mysteriously.

CHAPTER 4

It was a pitch-black night. There was a flash of lightning from time to time. Samlal was walking cautiously along the edge of a sewerage north of Bhartiyari Sarai with an electric torch in his hand and another man in tow to assist him. Whenever he heard the rustling of leaves, he became alert and started looking around. Upon reaching the northern window of a house, he started tapping on it.

The voice of an old woman came from inside. 'Who is it?'

'It's me,' whispered Samlal.

The old woman exclaimed, 'Babu, on a night such as this!' and opened the door.

Samlal was agitated. 'I had no choice,' he said. 'How many times have I told you to rent another place, but you never listen to me.' He got in and the old woman shut the door after him.

'Where is Naseeban?' he asked.

Naseeban was lying on the bed. She had a headache.

'Put aside your tantrums and come with me,' said Samlal. 'You are a lucky one. All the deputies and sub-deputies have become your admirers.'

The old woman asked, 'What about the SDO Nawab Saheb?'

'We all are his slaves, and you are no exception,' said Samlal.

But Naseeban was worried. 'Listen,' she said, 'Singh Ji is expected to visit me anytime soon, and if he gets to know, then we will be in trouble.'

'He won't,' said Samlal. 'Singh Ji has been sent far away on an assignment. Today, he went to Nawab Saheb grumbling about the nature of his job, but what can be accomplished by complaining?'

Naseeban refused still. 'For God's sake, please forgive me today,' she pleaded.

'Nawab Saheb is a powerful man,' said Samlal. 'Who dares disobey him? If I continue to work this way, and if he obliges me even with his one glance, I will be blessed.' Naseeban agreed that Samlal was gaining repute.

'Word is doing the rounds that you are gaining popularity. Clients are queuing up and people are full of praise for you,' she said.

Now Samlal grunted. 'Ignore those clowns! I couldn't care less, for I do not lack material comfort. All I want is that you somehow coax Nawab Saheb to bestow the title of Rai Bahadur upon me.'

'I am trying my best,' said Naseeban. 'He is very pleased with you, but he says that the higher authorities are a hindrance. Your enemies put a spanner in the works, challenging your credentials, questioning whether you are some zamindar,* and cooking up some cock and bull stories about you.'

Samlal: Why! I have managed to get a donation of Rs 2000 for the hospital and helped start a bank by the name of Seram. SDO Raghuvar Yadav, during his tenure, kept ranting but was able to set up only four societies. Whereas I managed to set up fifty societies, only after which the bank commenced its business. After much pleading with Babu Aidal Singh, I got a college built. Where else in the world would one find a mukhtar like me? Zamindar or not, how does it matter? I can arrange lakhs of rupees in no time! Birji–Firji† tried their best to build schools and colleges. Did I let them succeed? I have even managed to get a number of schools built named after Mahatma Gandhi—was anyone able to do any better than me? No one even knew about *khadi–khaddar‡* here. Who must be credited for all these?'

'How does any of this concern me?' asked Naseeban.

Samlal attempted to kiss and embrace her. 'I'm at your service, Naseeban,' he said. 'And willing to give my life for you.'

Naseeban was unyielding. She would not go to meet the Nawab.

---

* Landlord.
† Names of some rich men of Bihar Sharif.
‡ Refers to Mahatma Gandhi's movement to make Khadi handloom clothes.

Samlal touched her feet and pleaded, 'Please keep my honour and please don't make the situation more difficult for me, Naseeban.'

At this juncture, the old woman came gasping, 'Arré, Singh Ji has come. I have made some pretext of fetching the door key and come here to alert you.'

Both Samlal and Naseeban turned pale.

'Please save me!' croaked Samlal.

Naseeban: You never listen to me. Didn't I tell you that he would sneak in here at any time? Scurry and go straight out of the door, now.

Samlal: No, no, the shops are open on that side of the street.

Naseeban: Then go to the next room.

Samlal: Is anybody there?

Naseeban: Tafzula.

Samlal: Arré *baap re!** He will gossip about it with the whole town tomorrow.

Naseeban: Where else can I suggest you hide?

Samlal: What kind of room is on the right side?

Naseeban (smirking): It's the toilet.

Samlal swiftly entered the toilet, saying, 'It does not matter.'

Singh Ji came in. He looked greatly upset. He took the key from the old woman after shutting the windows and then entered the room. Holding her head, Naseeban got up and said, 'Come in, please sit down.'

---

* Oh my God.

Singh Ji asked furiously, 'Has Samlal come here?'

Naseeban: No, I don't know. I have had a headache since this morning.

Singh Ji: Swine! Today, he was bragging before me. While he himself is deceitful, he calls the whole world dishonest and corrupt. Come what may, I will deal with that bastard.

Rushing out of the room, he went to check Tafzula's room but found no one there. Then, he went towards the room in the courtyard; there too, he did not find anyone. He then turned around and glanced towards the toilet. He went there with a lantern and found Samlal sitting there in a corner, covering his face. He kicked him hard, cursing, 'Sala haramkhor!'*

Samlal sprang up shouting: Baap re!

Singh Ji (lifting his second foot): Shut up, son of a shrew (and taking out the revolver from his pocket, he pointed it towards him), be warned, all your bravery will come to an end here.

Saying this, he dragged him out holding his hand, and asked Naseeban, 'Now tell me where he appeared from?'

Samlal, the old woman and Naseeban, all started trembling in fear.

Naseeban: How do I know how he entered? Are these the attributes of a respectable man?

---

* Sisterfucker, parasite.

Old woman: I swear by God, I do not know anything. This young lady has been sick since morning and we all have been disturbed because of that.

Singh Ji (looking towards Samlal): Then Nawab Saheb must have sent him to spy on us. Today, I pleaded a great deal with him but he did not budge. He seems to be a wicked man. This motherfucker is after me, he thinks that he will earn a good reputation by doing all this, and this pimp (pointing towards Samlal) flatters him day and night, and is his spy. He can earn much more than this by indulging in some other unscrupulous activity.

Old woman: Mukhtar Saheb, you ruined everything. Why did you enter our place like a thief?

Singh Ji: Mukhtar Saheb, tell us the truth. How and why did you come here? Otherwise, I am going to kill you, and I don't care what the consequences may be.

Samlal (becoming calmer): I had a bet with my friend. He told me that Singh Ji visits Naseeban every day. I refused to believe him. On this, he said that the doors and windows of Naseeban's house are open in the evening, and I should go and see it for myself.

Singh Ji: The windows are always locked here, so how could you have entered?

Samlal: I did not know this, nor did my friend. I would have known this only if I had been here before.

Singh Ji: This is merely the justification of an accused; you're an expert in such matters.

Samlal (falling at Singh Ji's feet): May I die of leprosy if I lie!

Singh Ji (a little hesitant): I have heard that you take courtesans to clients and Naseeban, too, visits them. However, since both of you swore, I am convinced of the justification given. Please do not tell anyone about this incident. I had also come to catch both of you red-handed. Rumours that Naseeban is my keep are doing the rounds. It is a complete lie. Moreover, many people have told me, and I understand it completely, that this is why that obnoxious fellow sends me on field trips. Why does he engage in such drama? I would like to tell him that his cold behaviour doesn't affect me. I would like to ask him why I should be sent into the wilderness. But at the same time, I hesitate to say all this out of politeness.

Samlal: I have no idea what you are talking about. I am not involved in any of this.

Singh Ji: Why? I have heard that Sarbatiya is quite special to you. You have rented a separate accommodation for her and even have a son with her.

Samlal: Yes, I made a mistake once, but I'm not involved in pimping.

Singh Ji: Let bygones be bygones; whatever mistakes we have made have already been made, and nothing can be done about them, so let's forget about them. Let these not create rancour in our old friendship.

Samlal: Certainly, sir.

Giving her the key, Singh Ji then asked the old woman to open the door. She opened the door. Singh Ji and Samlal then went out, and the door was shut. Walking a little ahead, Singh Ji spoke, 'See, this SDO is a sly man; beware of him.'

Samlal: Yes, I keep my distance from him.

Singh Ji: Look, please do not talk about this incident with anyone else.

Samlal: No, not at all, sir. Rest assured.

CHAPTER 5

That night, while Babu Haldhar Singh was on his way back home, thoughts started floating in his mind of his encounter with Babu Samlal.

One moment, he thought, 'I have kicked him hard, and he happens to be a notorious backbiter and a pet of the SDO. He might inform the SDO about the incident and exaggerate it, which may start a quarrel.'

The next moment he thought, 'Samlal is a gentleman and has sworn not to tell anyone about the incident. Whatever I have heard about him seems to be a lie, as is the gossip about him being a pet of the SDO, so out of fear he would not tell anyone the story of his own humiliation.'

While he was still on the way, Singh wished to go back to Naseeban's house, but he remembered that she had had a headache since the morning. So he promptly returned home and went to sleep.

The next day, after a bout of indecision, he decided to set Samlal and the Nawab up and put tight security around Naseeban's residence.

Samlal could not forget the pain he had endured when Babu Haldhar Singh had kicked him. He was not embarrassed by it but had a great deal of seething anger inside of him against Babu Haldhar Singh.

Nawab Saheb had kept waiting anxiously for Naseeban's arrival the whole night. He sent his assistant several times to look for her, to find out whether she had arrived at Samlal's place. If so, she should be immediately called in. He also sent them to look for her out in the street in the hope that she might be on her way. At last, the assistant brought a cryptic handwritten note from Samlal. It read: 'My life has been barely spared; the enemy reached out to me and chased me away after thrashing me. I'm troubled at the moment. I will see you later.' Nawab Saheb felt dizzy reading his note and a sense of great disappointment shrouded his night.

The next morning, Babu Haldhar Singh reached Nawab Saheb's place with the devious intention of undercutting Samlal. After briskly exchanging greetings, Nawab Saheb asked, 'What's going on here? How are you doing?'

Singh Ji: I am doomed.

While discussing the cases, the conversation led to Mukhtar Samlal.

Nawab Saheb: Mukhtars make all things difficult. They do not let us know the whole truth about the matter and make fools of us.

Singh Ji: I wonder how they would face God! I had once tried to confront Kanhaiya Lal,* but he put the blame on us.

Nawab Saheb: What is our fault?

Singh Ji: The fact that, if the truth is told, we don't believe in it.

Nawab Saheb: Is that really the case? In reality, whenever there is a dispute, both sides are at fault—the complainant always tries to hide his own fault and the accused has to take all the blame on himself.

Singh Ji: That's right. If the accused does not lie out of fear, then he would be in trouble.

Nawab Saheb: Mukhtars, barring a few, have tainted the reputation of the profession, and its impact can be seen on the advocates and barristers who are arch-rivals in the court.

Singh Ji: No, these (mukhtars) are worse. There are very few whose conduct is righteous and can sustain public scrutiny. How many of them do you think must be God-fearing and thoughtful about righteous and honest conduct?

Nawab Saheb: Then, among the mukhtars and advocates, who is more genuine?

Singh Ji: There is not much difference in the conduct of the two. In fact, the new generation of mukhtars and advocates are believed to be way better than their older

---

* Name of a random senior official, maybe another mukhtar or a former SDO.

counterparts. From the older generation, there's hardly anyone who does not drink alcohol or toddy or does not keep a mistress.

Nawab Saheb: Samlal is among the old crop, but he seems to be a gentleman; he does not appear to be one of them.

Singh Ji: He is a silent killer.

Nawab Saheb (laughing out): Really?

Singh Ji: These days, most of them work at the court and the ones who wear a mark of sandalwood paste on their foreheads are dishonest and bribe-takers. Is there a kayastha who is not corrupt? Anyone who refrains from such wrongdoing gains nothing.

Nawab Saheb: And would you consider *babhans** as kayasthas too?

Singh Ji: That's right. However, is there a match for Babu Samlal among the babhans? Outwardly, he shines like burnished steel, but he has ruined many homes.

Nawab Saheb (taking great interest): Really?

Singh Ji: There is hardly anyone among his neighbours, irrespective of their caste, who has been spared or whose home he has not ruined in some way or another. These days, he is having an affair with the most beautiful *kaharin*† in town.

Nawab Saheb (knitting his brow and smiling a little): I didn't know that.

---

* A caste of landowning Brahmins.
† A woman of Kahar caste.

Singh Ji: This affair caused a big scandal. Her husband wanted to make a lot of noise about it, but Samlal is such a sly and lowly fellow that he got him jailed for one night with the help of Superintendent Saheb. Afterwards, her husband fled and has not returned to Bihar Sharif since. He got married to another woman after he was given fifty to one hundred rupees and was counselled by some people.

Nawab Saheb: So, Samlal does not have a wife?

Singh Ji: People say he had a beautiful wife, white as an English woman with beautiful eyes and hair. Once, some wicked people spread the rumour that he sent his wife to Ekli Saheb.

Nawab Saheb: Oh my God! Poor her, she must have felt mortified.

Singh Ji: What can I say about that? But we have investigated this matter seriously. The gossip about sending his wife was an absolute lie, but one night I saw Chamelwa, Samlal's wife, coming out of the Dak Bungalow with my own eyes.

Nawab Saheb: How can you conclude that she was beautiful if you saw her in the dark?

Singh Ji: I had seen her many times during the day. Who wouldn't want to sleep with her?

Nawab Saheb: So did you sleep with her?

Singh Ji (coyly): I don't want to invite any scandal or defamation. But it is true that I have had many affairs in my days.

Nawab Saheb was curious to know more about the beautiful Chamelwa but did not reveal his intentions while chatting with Singh Ji. Just then, his assistant brought a letter and Nawab Saheb started reading it. Meanwhile, Singh Ji's servant came looking for him, so he left, offering his salutations to Nawab Saheb.

In the mailbox, an anonymous letter had come from Ranchi. An anonymous person had viciously complained against Nawab Saheb. The bulk of the complaint was about Nawab Saheb's secret rendezvous with Naseeban. There were some complaints about him taking bribes as well. The British government was asking for an adequate response. The Nawab was paralysed. He slowly sank into his chair and brooded on the trouble that had befallen him.

CHAPTER 6

The morning brought an overcast sky at sunrise. Grey clouds thundered and rained all around the Nawab as he sat lost in thought. Much of the day was spent pondering, and it was only later in the afternoon that he sent for Samlal.

When Samlal arrived, he was confused to find Nawab Saheb in such a pensive mood. Certainly, the events had not unfolded as planned the previous night, but that couldn't be the reason for his distress.

He was still perplexed and considering whether he should sit down when Nawab Saheb spoke, 'Mukhtar Saheb, I have never seen such a place anywhere. I am being accused of something I am completely against. I am trying to stop the practice of bribery and doing my best within my capacity. But see how ungrateful people are!'

'What's the matter?' asked Samlal.

Nawab Saheb handed over the letter to Samlal and told him not to share the details with anyone.

Samlal: Not at all, sir. Do you expect such behaviour from me?

Samlal started reading it.

Nawab: I gave it to you to read because I consider you my confidant. Who else can I call my own?

After reading the letter, he said, 'All the people mentioned here are wrongly defamed.'

Nawab Saheb: Now what?

Samlal: It is evident that the letter has been sent by someone whose work has been hampered because of your actions.

Nawab Saheb: You mean the honorary magistrates . . .

Samlal: Maybe? However, what would they achieve by dragging Naseeban into this whole affair?

Nawab Saheb was pleased with this answer. 'Kudos Mukhtar Saheb! Now it all falls into place. Your experience as a mukhtar really counts.'

Samlal: No, sir, I possess a special secret trait—I get to the bottom of the truth. I have come across many people. I have even worked with Hasan Imam.* Most of them are against me, but they will not deny my adroitness. They merely have a greater name and fame, but they are no match for me.

'How did you find out the truth so quickly?' asked the Nawab.

---

* Syed Hasan Imam (1871–1933) was considered the best barrister of British India. He served as the president of the Indian National Congress.

'God has blessed me with the intellect to comprehend quickly,' said Samlal. 'But I also remembered something. Yesterday, while hiding at Naseeban's place, I overheard Babu Haldhar Singh's conversation. And what he said made me arrive at this conclusion.'

The Nawab was intrigued.

Samlal: What can I say? He spoke ill of you. He accused you of being corrupt yourself while you accuse others of being corrupt and other such vile talk.

Nawab Saheb: Is this the reason you didn't come last night? I was very disturbed. Today, this scoundrel has created another problem. How did you get out, then?

Samlal: I managed somehow to sneak out when he left. But it was too late by then, and Naseeban did not come.

'We must find a solution to this problem, Samlal,' said the Nawab. 'I will reply to this letter, but Singh Ji happens to be of the babhan caste. He is honest but he is also a crook with a great appetite, no less. The letter states that an investigation should be made and it should be supported by documentary evidence as well. Also, I must have written several letters to the landlords asking them to pay *chanda.** It appears that Singh Ji has collected them all.'

Samlal: Well, one of our men lives with Singh Ji at his house and is his confidant. He lets him open his coffer sometimes. He can do whatever he is asked to if he is promised something in return.

---

* Donation, a standard practice of collecting money for varied social or religious causes.

Nawab Saheb: This would not be sufficient. The wicked should be dealt with in equally wicked ways. When cooking the meat of a donkey, always use *reh*.*

Samlal: You are right. He is a thorn in the flesh that should be removed and thrown out.

Nawab Saheb: We will have to find the witnesses and some respected names.

Samlal: That's the difficult part.

Nawab Saheb: No, you can do everything. You will be one of the witnesses.

Samlal: No, sir, I am the one doing all the work. Moreover, I face scandal myself and I don't see any benefit for me in it.

Now the Nawab dropped his bait. 'I promise to make you Rai Bahadur before I leave, and if it does not happen, I'll chop off my hands. In return, you have to help me in this matter.'

Samlal: I'll do my best to the extent possible to help, sir.

---

* Salt.

CHAPTER 7

The scandal involving Nawab Saheb and Babu Haldhar Singh became the talk of the town. It was so talked about that the government decided to investigate both the officers—SDO Nawab Saheb and Circle Officer Babu Haldhar Singh. The commissioner of police, a certain Broadway Saheb, was appointed to investigate the matter.

Things got out of control. Even though Ram Kisun Singh was Haldhar Singh's trusted brother-in-law, the Nawab managed to lure him away with a juicy appointment as the sub-registrar at the secretariat. The promise of a high rank was too good to pass. Both Ram Kisun Singh, as well as various documents in the possession of Babu Haldhar Singh against Nawab Saheb, disappeared. Nawab Saheb also convinced a handful of the rich and eminently respectable people in the town, such as Ram Kisun Singh and Samlal, to become witnesses in the case. Babu Haldhar Singh was falsely implicated on

charges of bribery and fraud while Nawab Saheb got away
with his honour intact.

More mukhtars such as Bulaki Khan came forward to
help Nawab Saheb. Babu Haldhar Singh was dismissed
from service.

While leaving, Haldhar cursed everyone. 'You shall all
pay for it,' he shouted. 'Ram Kisun, Samlal, you will stay
childless throughout your life, and you will die a death
infested with worms.' He made a similar slew of unpleasant
remarks about Nawab Saheb and Bulaki Khan. Although
Haldhar Singh was no saint and had never been a man of
good conduct, such a great punishment meted out to him
despite his innocence was too much for him. He turned to
God and perhaps, that was the reason why justice came to
bite his detractors within three to four years of this incident.

After Babu Haldhar Singh's exit from Bihar Sharif,
Nawab Saheb lived in a state of bliss. So did Samlal and
Bulaki Khan, who had the time of their lives. Since Bulaki
Khan kept his distance from courtesans and alcohol,
Nawab Saheb used to often depend upon Samlal for these
arrangements.

Samlal would often plead with Nawab Saheb, saying,
'I have done all the work sir wanted me to do; there is
nothing that I have refused to do, and I continue to do so.
See how some wicked people of the town have now got
pamphlets printed making insinuations at me.'

Nawab Saheb: Which pamphlet?

Samlal handed over a pamphlet to the Nawab. 'Please
take a look,' he said.

But it was written in Devanagari and the Nawab could not read it. He asked it to be read out loud to him. Samlal started to read the pamphlet, which seemed to be a salacious recipe of sorts on how to become a Rai Bahadur.

Backbiting	:	4.5	masha[*]
Treason	:	1.25	masha
Dishonesty	:	2.5	masha
Total	:	8.25	masha
Plus Flattery	:	8.25	masha

Samlal was, of course, very angry. 'All these English-speaking people get their pen and ink from the well of freeloading. Then they run the well dry, blending it well with their moral turpitude. If that alone does not suffice, then combining it with pimping will certainly do the job,' he seethed.

Nawab Saheb only smiled. 'It's an abominable act,' he said gently. 'But don't worry, I'll take care of them all.'

The anonymity of the text bothered Samlal even more. 'The problem here is that it has neither the name of the author nor of the publisher, nor the printing press, and I fail to understand who can be behind this act. Moreover, if I lodge a police case, they will further humiliate me.'

Nawab Saheb: I'll hand over the matter to the police, they will investigate the matter.

---

[*] A unit of weight measurement used in olden days.

Samlal: No, please don't bother. Of late, everyone mocks me by asking whether news of my becoming Rai Bahadur has been published in the gazette. However, I am yet to get any confirmation about it from *Huzoor.* On 1 January, I read the gazette four times and did not find my name anywhere.

Nawab Saheb: If you can get Sarbatiya to visit me again, I swear it will be done.

Samlal: Oh my God! That night, when Huzoor slept with her when she was drunk and sleepy, she rained abuse on me on the following day. She forbade me to visit her for the next fifteen days. I kept rubbing my nose against the floor but to no avail.

Nawab Saheb: I will use the same trick again and go to her while she is still asleep. I made a mistake last time when I slept there till morning.

Samlal: I cannot disappoint Huzoor, but this time I request Huzoor to assure me and give me the news of my becoming a Rai Bahadur soon. Moreover, Naseeban keeps coming to Huzoor anyway.

---

* Sir.

CHAPTER 8

Samlal's happiness knew no bounds today.

It was the first day of April, the fourth month in the Gregorian calendar. In the morning, he received an envelope addressing him as 'Rai Bahadur Samlal' and hurried to meet with the Nawab to share the good news. But even before he could say anything, Nawab Saheb congratulated him on becoming Rai Bahadur and at the same time, informed him that he had been transferred out of Bihar Sharif. 'I feared that you would think that I was making false promises to you. But the Almighty has kept the honour of my words; otherwise, the people of this town would have made your life miserable after my departure,' he said.

Samlal drew his hands into a salute and joyfully showed him the letter.

Nawab Saheb: I, too, have received a similar letter.

He took out the letter and handed it over to him.

Samlal read the letter thrice. 'How precisely and elegantly it has been written!' he said.

Nawab Saheb: Yes! We could have written the same content in just two pages!

'They have addressed me as Rai Bahadur Samlal,' exulted the man.

The assistant came and announced that a large number of mukhtars and advocates had gathered outside the SDO office looking for Samlal to offer him their felicitations—the news of him being conferred with the title of Rai Bahadur and the transfer of the SDO had spread among the legal fraternity of Bihar Sharif.

Nawab Saheb and Samlal got up and came out to meet them all. Everyone present there was of the opinion that it was the right occasion to celebrate as Nawab Saheb was leaving and Samlal should repay him for being bestowed with the title of Rai Bahadur.

Samlal: Yes, of course! I have always been one of you.

Nawab Saheb: Certainly, Rai Bahadur! In the future, who knows where our destinies will take us?

They discussed the matter amongst themselves and it was decided that an announcement of this joyous news be made to the whole town. Babu Samlal handed over a paper to Mukhtar Samsundar Prasad, who used to participate actively on such occasions, with a note requesting the grocer and the *paanwala** to provide all the provisions needed for the feast. He made arrangements for lighting

---
* Betel leaf seller.

up the whole town, and distributed oil and lamps to every household at his own expense. It so happened that the mukhtars and advocates used to run a drama club in town, and they had arranged to perform a humorous play to mark the occasion. Samlal was delirious with joy and didn't pay a lot of attention to all the details. Everyone ate and drank, and the whole town was lit up. The play started at 8 p.m.

Before it began, the compère came to announce that it was a matter of great pleasure, that on this special occasion, they were presenting a play titled *Fool Bahadur*.

Samlal and the Nawab were delighted, and Nawab Saheb remarked, 'The title seems to be very amusing.'

Samlal: They act very well.

The Kiul station was in the background as soon as the curtain lifted.

Nawab: Wah! What a wonderful stage set they have created!

Samlal: Yes, sir! I myself have also contributed Rs 200 for the same.

The play began to be enacted on the stage. After a scene or two, Nawab Saheb wondered whether Samlal was aware of the contents of the play. Nawab Saheb was portrayed as an inspector in the play, while Samlal was portrayed as a lawyer by the name of Vrindavan and his wife's character in the play resembled Sarbatiya's.

Nawab Saheb then asked Samlal: Is there a script for the play? Please ask for it.

Samlal got the script for Nawab Saheb, who started reading it. When he read about Vrindavan being kicked in the toilet, he thought it to be a joke and read through the script. He found that after the banquet, Mohar Dakghar, a friend of Vrindavan, asked him to carefully examine the letter that brought him the news of being conferred the title of Rai Bahadur. When Vrindavan looked at the letter closely, he found a stamp from 'Ranchi Fools' Paradise' pasted on it. On removing it, he saw what he had missed earlier—'April Fool' written on it.

After reading, Nawab Saheb told Samlal: There seems to be something fishy here, do you have the letter that you have received?

Samlal: Yes, sir, I have it.

Samlal was trying to read his letter and when Nawab Saheb looked at the stamp on the envelope, he saw that it was from Shimla Fool's Paradise. He stood up saying, '*Shabash!*'* and left the theatre laughing. When Samlal opened the envelope and read the letter, he felt disappointed and angry. It was clearly typewritten in English:

Fool Bahadur

---

* Well done!

ACKNOWLEDGEMENTS

I'm grateful to Dhananjay Shrotriya for introducing me to *Fool Bahadur* and sending me its original Magahi manuscript, and to Chaitali Pandya for carefully reading my English translation of the novel and offering her valuable suggestions. My sincere gratitude to Milee Ashwarya, Moutushi Mukherjee and Aparna Abhijit at Penguin Random House India for their constant support during the publication of this landmark Magahi novel. A thank you to Ahlawat Gunjan for designing a fabulous cover.

Scan QR code to access the
Penguin Random House India website